modern readers stage 2

An American host family

Telma Guimarães Castro Andrade

To the famous writer and special friend
Eduardo Amos, who believed me.

Telma

2nd edition

Richmond

© TELMA GUIMARÃES CASTRO ANDRADE, 2005

Richmond

Diretoria: *Paul Berry*
Gerência editorial: *Sandra Possas*
Coordenação de revisão: *Estevam Vieira Lédo Jr.*
Coordenação de produção gráfica: *André Monteiro, Maria de Lourdes Rodrigues*
Coordenação de produção industrial: *Wilson Troque*

Projeto editorial: *Véra Regina A. Maselli*

Consultoria de língua inglesa: *Iraci Miyuki Kishi*
Preparação do texto: *Margaret Presser*
Assistência editorial: *Gabriela Peixoto Vilanova*
Revisão: *Denise Ceron*
Projeto gráfico de miolo e capa: *Ricardo Van Steen Comunicações e Propaganda Ltda./Oliver Fuchs*
Edição de arte: *Claudiner Corrêa Filho*
Ilustrações de miolo e capa: *Rogério Borges*
Diagramação: *Tânia Balsini*
Pré-impressão: *Helio P. de Souza Filho, Marcio H. Kamoto*
Impressão e acabamento: *Plenaprint Indútria Gráfica*
Lote. 795293
Cod. 12044823

Dados Internacionais de Catalogação na Publicação (CIP)
(Câmara Brasileira do Livro, SP, Brasil)

Andrade, Telma Guimarães Castro
  An American host family / Telma Guimarães Castro Andrade — 2. ed — São Paulo : Moderna, 2005 — (Modern readers ; stage 2)

  1. Inglês (Ensino fundamental) I. Título II. série.

04-8840   CDD-372.652

Índices para catálogo sistemático:
1. Inglês : Ensino fundamental   372.652

ISBN 85-16-04482-3

Reprodução proibida. Art. 184 do Código Penal e Lei 9.610 de 19 de fevereiro de 1998.

Todos os direitos reservados.

RICHMOND
SANTILLANA EDUCAÇÃO LTDA.
Rua Padre Adelino, 758, 3º andar — Belenzinho
São Paulo — SP — Brasil — CEP 03303-904
www.richmond.com.br
2024
Impresso no Brasil

Mateus is fifteen years old. He is an exchange student. It's his second day in the United States. He is from Brazil. He is staying with the Boorers family.

It's six fifteen in the morning. Mrs. Boorer is setting the table and everybody is up. Mateus is washing his face, brushing his teeth, combing his hair.

He is downstairs now. He says "good morning" to Mrs. Boorer, Valerie, Mr. Boorer, Steve, and their children: his "brother" Bill, who is his age, and his "sister" Ann, who is sixteen.

3

They are having breakfast now: milk and corn flakes, bacon and eggs, toast, raspberry jam and muffins.

"Humm, I really like these... What are these?" Mateus asks Mrs. Boorer.

"Muffins. They are very popular in the United States," she answers.

Bill and Ann are laughing.

"Don't you have muffins in your country?" they ask the boy.

"Well, I don't think so. How do you spell it?" he wants to know.

"M - U - F - F - I - N - S!" Mr. Boorer spells out slowly.

Mrs. Boorer is glad. She thinks it's really good when somebody appreciates her recipes.

They are at Dixon High School now.

Mateus is very anxious. He meets many people from Mexico, Ecuador, Argentina, France, Portugal, and Italy. They are foreign students like he is.

The school is very different from his school in Brazil. It's much bigger, with a swimming pool and, best of all, there are partitions between the classrooms.

He doesn't have to buy any books. The school lends the books to the students. At the end of the year, the students must give them back. They can't write in the books, of course.

'That's very unusual. Why don't our schools do the same?' he wonders.

There's nice music playing all around. He likes it. It's nice.

'You can relax', he thinks.

Mrs. White is Mateus's English teacher. She is sweet and patient.

Mrs. White introduces the new student.

"This is our friend Mr. Lopes, from São Paulo, Brazil," she starts. "Well, how do you like it here, Mateus?"

Mateus explains it's his first week in Conyers, Georgia. It's his first day at school too. He says he wants to know the American way of life and expects he can tell interesting things about his country. He hopes to make many friends at school.

After the English class, Mateus is introduced to another teacher, Mr. Black, who teaches American Literature. Mateus thinks those last names are very strange.

'They are names of colors!'

The students must read some poems.

Mateus is a little nervous. He doesn't know that poet, Walt Whitman. The poem is long and he is afraid of making too many mistakes in his manner of speech. "Go on!" Mr. Black encourages the student. "You must feel the poetry, my son. Poetry is like music, it fills your heart with love, tenderness and sometimes with sadness."

Mateus starts reading.

'It's not easy being a foreign student!' he thinks to himself.

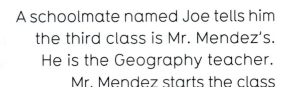

A schoolmate named Joe tells him the third class is Mr. Mendez's. He is the Geography teacher. Mr. Mendez starts the class telling the students that Colombia is the biggest producer of coffee in South America.

"Do you agree, Mr. Lopes?" he asks the boy.

"No, sir. As far as I know, Brazil is the first one. Brazil produces twenty per cent of the world coffee production and Colombia produces fourteen per cent."

"Very good. You are right. We can exchange information about our countries, don't you agree?"

Mateus thinks so. He loves it when people ask him questions about his country.

There is a thirty-minute break until the next class begins.

Some of the students walk to the library, others stand in the corridor, or go to the toilets, drink some water or just keep on talking to their friends.

Bill and Ann take Mateus to the school music hall. They sit down on the stairs and relax for a time. Mateus thinks it's a cool thing!

Fourth class.

The students have to leave the class and go to the gym.

Mateus is surprised! 'Dancing classes? How come? What for?'

The teacher says they must take square dance.

Mrs. Carter introduces herself to the students. The students must do the same.

"Hello! My name is Susan Clifford. What's your name?" a blond girl with blue eyes starts the conversation.

"Hi! My name is Mateus Lopes and I'm from Brazil. It's my first dance. Please, help me!" he asks.

"Of course," answers Susan.

The girl is very patient. She doesn't know how to dance either.

They laugh a lot when they stumble together.

"What kind of dance is this?" Mateus asks her.

"Boot Scooten Boogie," Susan tells him.

Susan is very cute. She helps Mateus all the time.

'I hope she can give me a little help next class!' he thinks.

Fifth class.

Bill takes Mateus to the lab. There's a nursery right beside the lab. It's the first time he sees a nursery in a school.

Mrs. Jones gives the Biology books to the students. She shows the students Mr. Jack's skeleton.

Everybody laughs.

Mrs. Jones is funny. Mateus likes her.

Mr. Jack is a very weird skeleton. He has a Chicago Bulls' cap on the skull.

It's twelve fifteen.

Mateus is at the cafeteria now.

The students pick up their trays and choose their meal. Mateus sits between Bill and Ann.

Bill has chocolate milk, salad, spaghetti, and, for dessert, strawberry jelly.

Ann prefers orange juice, salad, rice, fried chicken, and, for dessert, an apple.

Mateus asks for rice, beans, and a steak, his favorite food in Brazil.

Bill and Ann tell him they don't usually have steak in a cafeteria, only at restaurants. They also tell him that rice and beans are not so popular in the United States.

"And it's too expensive!" they say.

So, Mateus decides to ask for iced tea, salad, rice, fried chicken and...

"An apple a day keeps the doctor away," Ann tells him an American proverb.

"OK. An apple then."

Mateus likes the meal... But he longs for Brazilian food.

Physical Education is the last class. They have double lessons today.

There are only boys in this lesson.

They have to learn some basketball rules.

The coach's nickname is Big Bull. He's really tall.

They must change clothes, take off their jeans, T-shirts and put on the uniform: navy blue shorts, yellow T-shirts, and sneakers.

Now, they're ready to play. They're "The Bulls".

As soon as the bell rings, the classes are over.

Some students go back home by car, with their parents. Mateus, Bill, and Ann take the school bus to go back home.

Bill has the front door key. Mr. and Mrs. Boorer usually get home late. They work downtown Atlanta and take a long way driving back home.

The kids are hungry.

"I bet everybody here is hungry!" Bill says.

"I am!" Ann opens the freezer.

"Me too!" Mateus is still a little shy.

Bill has an idea. He can try to make some muffins for his new friend.

Everybody likes the idea.

Bill looks for his mother's book of recipes. He starts to teach Mateus how to make the muffins.

*Muffins

Put in a mixing bowl:
    1 1/2 cup of flour
    1/2 cup of sugar
    2 teaspoons of baking powder
    1/2 teaspoon of salt

Add: 1/4 cup of soft shortening
      1 egg
      1/2 cup of milk

Mix all the ingredients with a fork and stir until they are blended. Fill greased muffin cups 2/3 full. Bake until golden brown. Bake at 250℃ for 35 to 40 minutes.

Yield: 12 medium muffins.

The muffins are ready now and they are delicious! Bill and Mateus go to the living room and turn on the TV. While they watch TV they eat the muffins.
It's five thirty and their parents aren't home yet. The kitchen is a mess.
Ann calls the boys. She needs some help.
Mateus asks his friends about the maid.
"She can come tomorrow and clean it, can't she?"

Atenção: Se você quiser preparar as receitas apresentadas nesta história, procure observar as medidas de segurança necessárias, principalmente ao acender o fogo.

Ann and Bill tell him they don't have a maid. Everybody must help with the housework. They have to cook, wash, dry, clean their bedrooms, and make the beds to help their mother.

Mateus tells them in Brazil it's quite different. Then he figures out it's not so different. In fact most people in Brazil don't have maids. They must do everything by themselves.

They go on talking while they clean up that mess.

After that they start doing their homework.

It's almost seven.

The telephone rings. The Boorers are going to arrive late. They have a meeting and they are coming back at around nine.

Ann decides to fix hot dogs so her parents can have some when they come back home. She opens the freezer and takes out the sausages but she discovers there is no bread.

"We can order a pizza!" she says.

"Maybe we can make a Brazilian recipe!" Mateus suggests.

Ann and Bill agree. They want to taste Brazilian food.

Mateus goes upstairs and brings down a magazine.

"Here there are some recipes from Brazil. I can try this one: cheese empadinha," Mateus says.

"We can help you!" the kids are curious.

"That's okay!" Mateus is anxious.

It's the first time he cooks. He hopes he succeeds.

Cheese empadinha

Dough: 1 stick of margarine
1 1/2 cup of flour
1/2 tablespoon of baking powder
2 egg yolks
a pinch of salt
1 tablespoon of oil
5 full tablespoons of milk
salt to taste

Filling: 3 eggs
1/2 cup of grated cheese
1/2 cup of milk

Mix all ingredients for the dough. Put some portions in small greased forms and stretch the dough from bottom to top. Mix the filling together and lay one full tablespoon of filling on the dough. Bake them at 250℃ for 45 minutes until golden.

Yield: 30 medium empadinhas.

The cheese empadinhas are finally ready.

They are setting the table when Mr. and Mrs. Boorer enter the dining room.

They are very tired but they are happy. A good smell comes from the kitchen.

"What are these little things, Mateus? They smell good!" they are very curious.

The boy is very proud of himself. The empadinhas seem to be delicious.

They sit for dinner.

The cheese empadinhas are absolutely fantastic.

"I really like these... What do you call them, 'son'?" Mr. Boorer asks Mateus.

"Cheese empadinhas, 'dad'. A dough filled with grated cheese" Mateus explains. "Empadinhas are very popular in Brazil. They can be filled with hearts of palm, shrimp, chicken or cheese. You don't have empadinhas in the USA, do you?" he asks his host family.

"Well, I don't think so. How do you spell it?" asks Mrs. Boorer.

"E – M – P – A – D – I – N – H – A – S," Mateus spells out slowly.

Ann and Bill don't even repeat it. They can't stop eating!

"Oh, I'm full!" says Mr. Boorer.

"Would you help me with the dishes?" Mrs. Boorer asks for help.

Mr. Boorer takes the dishes off the table while the kids help their mother.

17

After doing the dishes, they sit near the fireplace and turn on the TV. Ann and Bill start to argue. Ann wants to watch a soap opera but Bill prefers "Tales from the Crypt".

'They are just like my brothers in Brazil!' Mateus smiles.

The Boorers turn on to CNN news. The weather forecast says it will probably snow the following day.

Mateus is very excited. He wants to see snow. He wonders what it looks like.

He says "good night" to the Boorers.

"God bless you!" they tell their Brazilian "son".

"God bless you too, 'Mom and Dad'!" he says.

Mateus is tired. His "brothers" are still arguing downstairs.

'Many things are different... But not so many!' he thinks as he gets into bed, before he starts to pray.

18

KEY WORDS

The meaning of each word corresponds to its use in the context of the story (see page number, 00)

a lot (11) muito, bastante
absolutely (17) absolutamente
add (14) acrescentar
afraid (7) com medo
after (7) depois
agree (8) concordar
almost (15) quase
anxious (5) ansioso
any (5) nenhuma, alguma
argue (18) discutir
around (5) por volta
arrive (15) chegar
as soon as (12) logo que
ask (4) pedir; perguntar
bake (14) assar
baking powder (14) fermento em pó
be over (12) terminar, acabar
beans (11) feijão
before (18) antes
begin (8) começar
bell (12) campainha
between (5) entre (dois)
bigger (5) maior
blend (14) misturar
blond (9) loira
bottom (16) fundo
break (4) intervalo
breakfast (4) café da manhã
bring down (15) trazer para baixo
brush (3) escovar

bull (11) búfalo
buy (5) comprar
by themselves (15) sozinhos
cafeteria (11) refeitório, cantina
call (14) chamar
can (5) poder
cap (11) boné
change clothes (12) trocar de roupa
cheese (15) queijo
chicken (11) frango
choose (11) escolher
classrooms (5) salas de aula, classes
clean (14) limpar
clean (up) (15) limpar
coach (12) treinador
comb (3) pentear
come (9) vir
cook (15) cozinhar
country (4) país
cup (14) xícara; forminha
cute (10) bonita
dancing classes (9) aulas de dança
dessert (11) sobremesa
dining room (17) sala de jantar
dinner (17) jantar
dish (17) prato (comida)
do the dishes (18) lavar a louça
double lesson (12) aula dupla
dough (16) massa

downstairs (3) andar de baixo
downtown (13) centro da cidade
dry (15) secar
egg yolk (16) clara de ovo
either (10) também
encourage (7) animar; encorajar
everybody (3) todo mundo
exchange (8) trocar
exchange student (3) aluno de intercâmbio
expect (6) esperar, aguardar
expensive (11) caro
explain (6) explicar
eyes (9) olhos
feel (7) sentir
figure out (15) imaginar; calcular
fill (7) encher, preencher
filling (16) recheio
fireplace (18) lareira
fix (15) preparar
flour (14) farinha
food (11) comida
foreign student (5) aluno estrangeiro
fork (14) garfo
form (8) fôrma
fried (11) frito
give (4) dar
glad (7) contente, feliz
go (12) ir
go back (7) voltar
go on (7) continuar
golden brown (14) dourado
grated cheese (16) queijo ralado
greased (14) untada
gym (9) ginásio de esportes
happy (17) feliz
heart (7) coração

heart of palm (tree) (17) palmito
help (10) ajuda; ajudar
home (12) casa (lar)
hope (6) esperança; esperar
hot (15) quente
housework (15) serviço (de casa)
how (4) como
hungry (13) com fome
iced tea (11) chá gelado
introduce (6) apresentar
juice (11) suco
just (8) exatamente; apenas
keep (8) manter
keep on (8) continuar
key (13) chave
kids (13) garotos
kitchen (14) cozinha
know (4) saber; conhecer
lab (10) laboratório
last (7) última
last name (7) sobrenome
late (11) tarde
laugh (4) rir
learn (12) aprender
leave (9) sair; deixar
lend (5) emprestar
library (8) biblioteca
like (14) gostar; como
little (7) um pouco; pequeno
living room (14) sala de estar
long (7) comprido
long for (11) sentir saudade; ansiar por
long way (13) longa distância
look (13) parecer
look for (13) procurar
look like (18) parecer-se com
magazine (15) revista
maid (14) empregada

many (5) muitos
maybe (15) talvez
meal (11) refeição
meet (5) encontrar; conhecer
meeting (15) reunião
mess (14) bagunça
mistake (7) erro
mixing bowl (14) tigela para misturar
most people (15) a maioria das pessoas
much (5) muito
must (5) dever
navy blue (12) azul-marinho
near (18) perto
new (6) novo
news (18) notícia, noticiário
next (8) próximo
nice (5) agradável; bela
nursery (10) enfermaria
only (11) somente
open (13) abrir
order (15) pedir, encomendar
parents (12) pais
people (5) pessoas
pick up (11) pegar, apanhar
pinch (16) pitada
poetry (7) poesia
pray (18) orar
producer (8) produtor
proud (17) orgulhoso
proverb (11) provérbio
put (12) colocar, pôr
put on (12) vestir
quite (15) bem; totalmente
raspberry jam (4) geléia de framboesa
ready (12) pronto
really (4) realmente

recipe (4) receita
relax (5) relaxar
rice (11) arroz
ring (12) tocar
rule (12) regra
sadness (7) tristeza
salt (14) sal
same (5) mesmo
sausage (15) salsicha
say (3) dizer; contar
schoolmate (8) colega, companheiro de escola
seem (17) parecer
set the table (3) pôr a mesa
shrimp (17) camarão
shy (13) tímido
skull (11) crânio
slowly (4) lentamente
small (16) pequena
smell (17) cheiro
smile (18) sorrir
sneakers (12) tênis
snow (18) neve
so (4) tão
so many (18) tantas
soap opera (18) novela
soft shortening (14) banha em temperatura ambiente
some (6) alguns; uns
somebody (4) alguém
sometimes (7) às vezes
spell (out) (4) soletrar
square dance (9) quadrilha
stairs (9) escadas
stand (8) ficar em pé
start (6) iniciar, começar
stay with (3) morar; passar temporada
steak (11) bife

stick (16) tablete, barra
still (13) ainda
stir (14) agitar
strawberry jelly (11) gelatina de morango
stretch (16) esticar
stumble (10) tropeçar, topar com
succeed (15) ser bem-sucedido
sugar (14) açúcar
sweet (6) simpática; encantadora
swimming pool (5) piscina
tablespoon (16) colher de sopa
take (7) levar; pegar
take off (12) tirar; despir
take out (15) tirar
tall (12) alto
taste (15) provar
teach (7) ensinar
teaspoon (14) colher de chá
teeth (3) dentes
tell (6) contar, dizer
tenderness (7) ternura
thing (6) coisa
think (4) achar; pensar
time (7) vez; hora; tempo
tired (17) cansado
toast (4) torrada
together (10) juntos
toilet (8) toalete, banheiro
top (16) em cima
tray (11) bandeja
try (13) experimentar, tentar
T-shirt (12) camiseta
turn on (14) ligar
unusual (5) raro; inusitado
until (8) até
up (3) em pé, levantado
usually (11) geralmente
walk (8) andar, caminhar
want (4) querer

wash (3) lavar
watch (14) assistir
water (8) água
weather forecast (18) previsão do tempo
weird (11) estranho
what (4) o que
when (4) quando
while (6) enquanto
who (3) quem
why (5) por que
wonder (5) perguntar-se
work (13) trabalhar; trabalho
year (3) ano
yet (14) ainda
yield (14) rendimento

Expressions

all around (5) por todos os lados
American way of life (6) estilo de vida norte-americano
as far as I know (8) que eu saiba
best of all (5) melhor de tudo
God bless you! (18) Deus o abençoe!
How come? (9) Como?
How do you like it here? (6) Você gosta daqui?
I'm full! (17) Estou satisfeito!
It's a cool thing! (9) É uma coisa legal!
manner of speech (7) modo de falar, pronunciar
school music hall (9) salão de música da escola
Well, I don't think so (4) Bem, eu acho que não.
What for? (9) Para quê?

ACTIVITIES

A. Answer the questions.

1. What's the main character's name?
2. How old is he?
3. Where is he from?
4. Who is he staying with?
5. What are his "brothers" names?

B. Answer the questions.

1. What are they having for breakfast?
2. Why is the school different from Mateus's school in Brazil?
3. Who is Mateus's English teacher?
4. Which country is the biggest producer of coffee?

C. Check the correct alternative.

1. They must take
   a) jazz lessons.
   b) opera lessons.
   c) square dance lessons.

2. Mrs. Jones shows the students
   a) the nursery room.
   b) Mr. Jack's skeleton.
   c) her new high-heeled shoes.

3. In the cafeteria
   a) Mateus decides to have iced tea, salad, rice, fried chicken, and an apple.
   b) Mateus decides to have rice, beans, and a steak.
   c) Mateus decides to have orange juice, salad, rice, fried chicken, and an apple.

D. Answer the questions.

1. How do Mateus, Bill, and Ann come back home?
2. Where do the kids' parents work?
3. What does Bill decide to make in the kitchen?
4. What must the kids do to help their mother?

E. True or False?

1. Ann decides to order some pizza.
2. Mateus is an exchange student from Brazil.
3. Mateus knows the recipe by heart.
4. The cheese empadinhas are fantastic.
5. Mrs. Boorer doesn't ask for help.
6. After doing the dishes they go to bed.
7. They sit near the fireplace and turn on the TV.

F. Answer the questions.

1. What are the empadinhas filled with?
2. Why do Bill and Ann start to argue?
3. What does the weather forecast say about the weather?
4. What does Mateus say to the Boorers before going to bed?